The Lost Little Bird

David McPhail

GODWINBOOKS

Henry Holt and Company
New York

To my darlin' granddaughters:

Kristyn, Adeline, Kaitlyn, and, last but not least, Avery!

Henry Holt and Company, *Publishers since 1866*
Henry Holt® is a registered trademark of Macmillan Publishing Group, LLC
120 Broadway, New York, NY 10271
mackids.com

Library of Congress Control Number: 2020910173
ISBN 978-1-250-22291-6

Our books may be purchased in bulk for promotional, educational,
or business use. Please contact your local bookseller or the Macmillan
Corporate and Premium Sales Department at (800) 221-7945 ext. 5442
or by email at MacmillanSpecialMarkets@macmillan.com.

Design by Kathleen Breitenfeld and Mallory Grigg
The illustrations for this book were created with pen and umber ink on
Strathmore illustration board, and then colored with watercolor paint.
First edition, 2021
Printed in China by RR Donnelley Asia Printing Solutions Ltd., Dongguan City, Guangdong Province

1 3 5 7 9 10 8 6 4 2

A little bird flew into a tree and bumped his head.

The little bird felt all jumbled up.
He couldn't even remember what kind of bird he was.

But the little bird was determined to find out.

Maybe I'm a robin, he thought.

Perhaps he was an eagle.

Could I be a crow? the little bird wondered.

An owl tried to help by asking the little bird some questions.

But the owl flew away before
the little bird could answer.

The little bird spotted an egret standing in a pond and flew down to join her.

But he soon discovered that he was **NOT** an egret.

Nor was he a sandpiper!

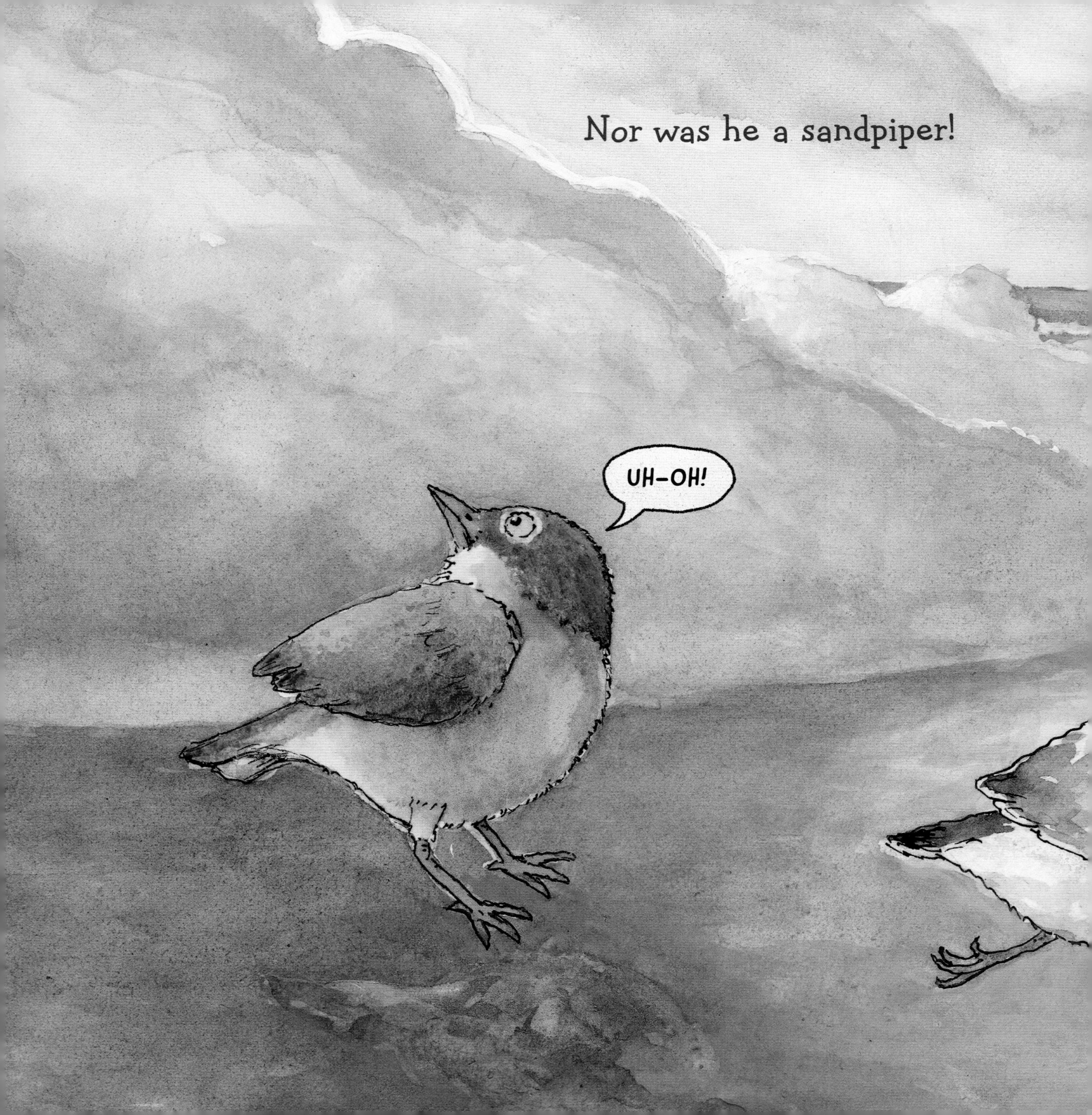

The answer, again, was **NO**.

But the little bird knew he was **NOT** a chicken.

He tried pecking wood . . .

The little bird was sad and discouraged.

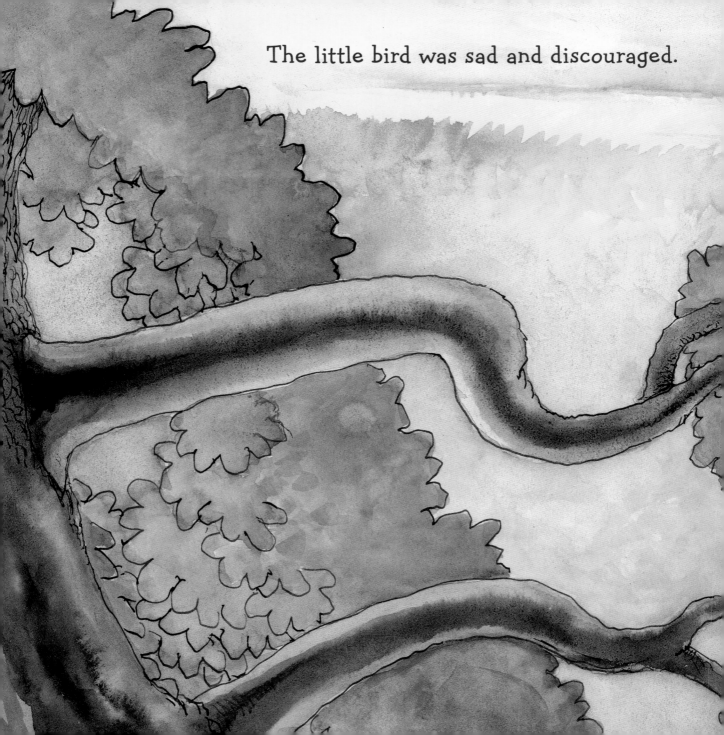

He flew down and landed on the rim of a birdbath.

As he sat there, the little bird
was joined by another bird.

"Hello," she said. "Who are you?"

"I don't know," the little bird replied.

"I bumped my head and forgot. I don't even know what KIND of bird I am!"

"You are a bluebird, like me," she told the little bird.

The little bird was happy.

Now he knew what kind of bird he was.
"You can come to my house,"
said his companion.

So the little bird did.

And he stayed for a long, long time.